Show and Tell

Elvira Woodruff

illustrated by
Denise Brunkus

Holiday House / New York

Library of Congress Cataloging-in-Publication Data
Woodruff, Elvira.
Show-and-tell / by Elvira Woodruff : illustrated by Denise Brunkus.—1st ed.
p. cm.
Summary: Andy's offerings for show-and-tell always seem to bore
his kindergarten class until one day he finds a magic bottle of
bubbles that temporarily transports all of them on an aerial
adventure.
ISBN 0-8234-0883-3
[1. Bubbles—Fiction. 2. Schools—Fiction.] I. Brunkus, Denise,
ill. II. Title.
PZ7.W8606Sh 1991   90-23588   CIP   AC
[E]—dc20

For our favorite teatime two, Marian and Pat,
and for all the show-and-tells to come.

E.W. and D.B.

Andy never had anything good for show-and-tell.

Daniel always had something big.

Megan always had something fancy.

Peter always had something scary.

Emma usually had something hairy.

But Andy never seemed to have anything interesting at all. Once he brought in a paper clip that no one wanted to look at.

Another time, he brought in a shoelace that he had found. It looked so old that Andy thought it might be the oldest shoelace in the world. No one else seemed to think so.

When Andy brought in his favorite fork, the one with the bent handle, even Mrs. Applelarney yawned.

Emma Oletti just shook her head. "You've got the worst show-and-tells in the whole class, maybe the whole school," she told him.

One day, on his way to school, Andy saw something interesting sticking up out of the grass.

He reached down and picked up a blue bottle with a picture of a little boy blowing bubbles on it. The words underneath the picture said: CAUTION: BUBBLES MAY CAUSE TROUBLES.

Andy couldn't read the words, but he liked the look of the letters.

"This will be perfect for show-and-tell," he thought, and he put the bottle in his book bag.

Andy was the first person picked for show-and-tell. He proudly held up the blue bottle. "It's probably the oldest bottle of bubbles in the world," Andy told the class.

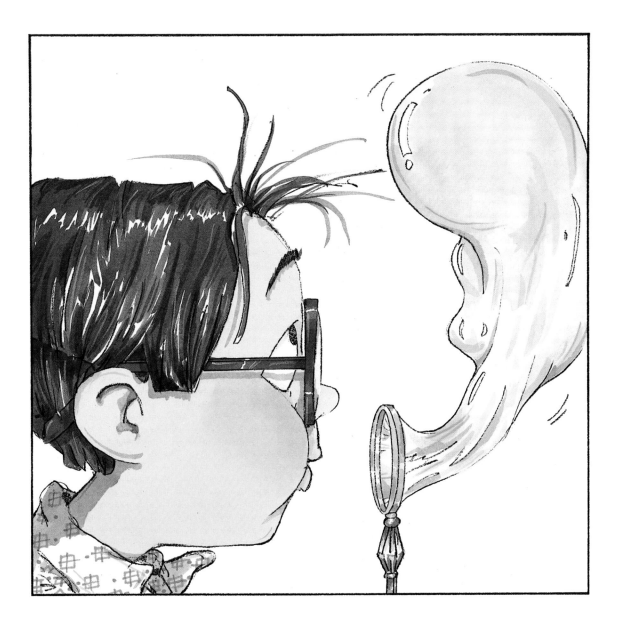

"It's probably so old, the bubbles don't work," Emma Oletti said with a smirk.

"If they don't work," Andy thought, "I'll never show up for show-and-tell again." He pulled the bubble wand out of the bottle and lightly blew through it.

A great, glorious bubble floated to the ceiling. It
bounced off the bulletin board before landing on Mrs. Applelarney's head.